Dedicated to Grandma's favorite littles! When waves crash down around you, take a breath and look for the treasures the waves delivered. You've got this!

Randee Nielson

This book is dedicated to my wonderful children, Daniel and Sage. And to all those who have helped me see the creative and joyous part of life's sometimes bumpy journey.

Curt Snarr

Seek Your Treasure

This book is given with love to...

To:

_____

From:

_____

BEYOND
the HEDGES

The Most Curious Adventure
of Hedgehog *and* Mouse

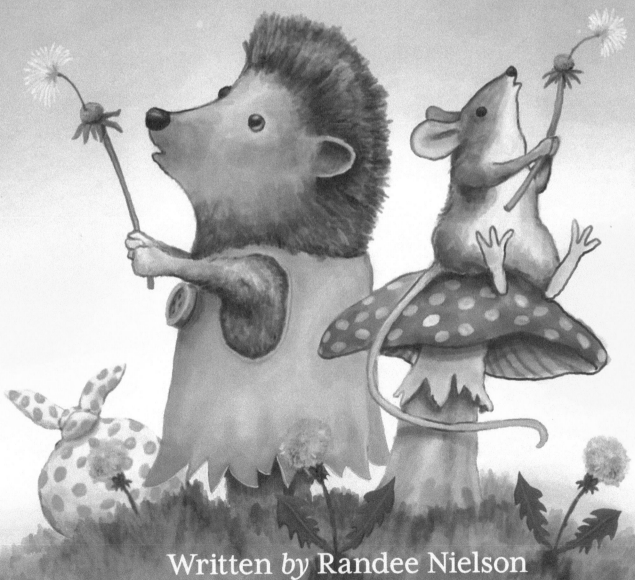

Written *by* Randee Nielson

Illustrated *by* Curt Snarr

Mouse is a dreamer. Everybody knows it.
Mouse finds unexpected surprises everywhere he goes.
Or maybe unexpected surprises find Mouse.
Nobody knows for sure.

Let Your Dreams be Magical

When he was just a squeaky little mouse, his mama would hold him close and softly whisper in his ear, "Sleep deep with magical dreams, for one day your dreams will find you." She tucked him into his cozy bed, and left him dreaming in the night-light of his own imagination.

Mouse grew. And so did his dreams.
Hedgehog, being a very good friend,
listened to his adventures, and wished she
could go on an adventure too.
She blew a dandelion wish into the air.

Dream Big!
Wish Big!

*Hedgehog began to write herself
some notes, that she would slip into
her pocket to read for later.*

Take Time to Imagine

Keep Moving Steadily
Along Your Path

One sunny day, Hedgehog saw a curious fellow moving at a snails pace toward her. Snail Mail didn't arrive very often, and she was delighted there was a letter addressed to her! Wiping a bit of slime from her note, she read:

" Would you join me on my next grand adventure ?"

Check: ☒ Yes or ☐ No

Your friend,
Mouse

Opportunities arrive in their own due time!

Hedgehog was happy that she had dared
to make her dandelion wish. She had patiently
prepared for her wish to come true,
and her bag was already packed!

Wishes hold special
magic for those
who prepare!

And the adventure began...

MS. HEIDI HEDGEHOG

Not sure when I'll Be Back...

Gone on an ADVENTURE

The journey began in a little boat on the water. Hedgehog paddled while Mouse studied the horizon and gave important directions.

Together, they stayed on course, letting their light and the waves lead the way.

Even if you don't know exactly where you're going, start anyway!

Hold On... When Life Gets Bumpy

They experienced many bumps along the way, but in the end, the bumps got them exactly where they were meant to be.

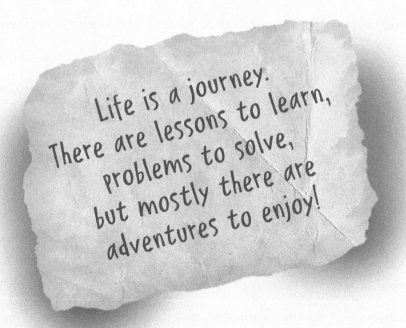

Life is a journey.
There are lessons to learn,
problems to solve,
but mostly there are
adventures to enjoy!

Mouse and Hedgehog's boat washed upon the shore
of a sparkling, aqua blue ocean as big
as the whole wide world! The giant waves
delivered curious and magical treasures to them...

Hedgehog listened to the tales of the Ocean
as it echoed in a shell while Mouse studied the
messages of wise people from long ago.

Sometimes
change comes
in waves to
lead you in new
directions.

Discover Unexpected Surprises

Take Time to
Listen to Your Heart

Mouse and Hedgehog took moments
along the way to watch the clouds
float across the sky. They talked,
shared stories, and laughed so hard
until no sound came out.
That's what friends do!

Taking time out is
by no means a
waste of time.

Sometimes new experiences came out of NOWHERE! Mouse suddenly took an unexpected leap of faith. Hedgehog put away her fears and followed him.

Mouse and Hedgehog experienced highs and lows along their journey, but during one of their highs they learned that the ground below looks like a large, patchwork quilt!

Sometimes you just have to take a leap of faith

And on one of their lows, they learned
that there would always be others
to help guide them on their journey
by lighting the way.

One new friend with a glowing light
led them to a rare and magical
four-leaf clover.

Always shine bright,
providing light to help
guide others on
their journey.

Millions of sparkling fireflies whispered the secret of the shamrock: "Friends are like four-leaf clovers, hard to find but lucky to have."

They smiled, happy they had a friend to share their journey with.

As they continued their journey,
Mouse recognized an old sign that had
once been near his field.
"That's strange", said Mouse.

They suddenly realized that they had gone
wherever they wanted to go, and yet
their journey had led them back home.

The best
journey
takes you
home.

TO WHEREVER
YOU WANT
TO GO

Her journey over, Hedgehog removed a whole pocketful of the lessons she had learned all along the way. She placed each note one-by-one into her slightly worn travel journal. She pressed the special four-leaf clover between two pages, and closed her book.

Sometimes you just have to take a leap of faith

Even if you don't know exactly where you're going, start any way!

Sometimes change comes in waves to lead you in new directions.

Taking time out is by no means a waste of time.

Always shine bright,
Providing light to help
guide others on
their journey.

The best
journey
takes you
home.

TRAVEL
JOURNAL
Ms Hedgehog

Opportunities arrive
in their own
due time!

Dream Big!
Wish Big!

The beginning of a wonderful partnership

Once upon a time a man named Curt Snarr walked into a gift shop and asked to speak to the owner. He carried with him a portfolio of his art.

The owner Randee Nielson, came to the front and saw the delightful artwork, falling in love with the colors and softness in the art. She liked the story and messages she could see in the art.

They struck up a great friendship. That day, Randee left work, having agreed to write the story to go with the illustrations, and Curt left with the goal to fill each page with beauty. With her whimsical writing and his lovable characters, they wove a tale of adventure, lessons learned and most of all, the friendship between Hedgehog and Mouse.

About the Author

Randee Nielson, known as Grandma Randee to some awesome kids, has owned and operated a gift and home decor business for over thirty years. Her notes of wisdom can empower every child to find the good in life's journey, even when things get bumpy or waves crash down around us.

About the Illustrator

Curt Snarr, illustrator extraordinaire, has a love for all things magical, which is obvious in the details of his art. He is a busy and successful graphic designer by day and illustrator by night, bringing pleasure to the child in all of us.